MONEY

Make It • Spend It • Save It

MW00905008

J. E. BOGART

MONEY

Make It · Spend It · Save It

Cartoons by
Teco Guerreiro

Scholastic Canada Ltd.
Toronto New York London Auckland Sydney
Mexico City New Delhi Hong Kong

Scholastic Canada Ltd.
175 Hillmount Road, Markham, Ontario, Canada L6C 1Z7
Scholastic Inc.
555 Broadway, New York, NY 10012, USA
Scholastic Australia Pty Limited
PO Box 579, Gosford, NSW 2250, Australia
Scholastic New Zealand Limited
Private Bag 94407, Greenmount, Auckland, New Zealand
Scholastic Ltd.
Villiers House, Clarendon Avenue, Leamington Spa,
Warwickshire CV32 5PR, UK

Cover photo by Paul Isaac
Coin designs courtesy of the Royal Canadian Mint

Canadian Cataloguing in Publication Data

Bogart, Jo Ellen, 1945–
Money : make it, spend it, save it

ISBN 0-590-24858-8

1. Finance, Personal — Juvenile literature. 2. Money — Juvenile literature. 3. Money-
making projects for children — Juvenile literature. I. Guerreiro, Teco. II. Title.

HG179.B626 2001   j332.024   C00-932492-5

Text copyright © 2001 by Jo Ellen Bogart.
Illustrations copyright © 2001 by Scholastic Canada Ltd.
All rights reserved.

No part of this publication may be reproduced or stored in a retrieval system,
or transmitted in any form or by any means, electronic, mechanical, recording,
or otherwise, without written permission of the publisher,
Scholastic Canada Ltd., 175 Hillmount Rd., Markham, Ontario, Canada L6C 1Z7.
In the case of photocopying or other reprographic copying, a licence must be obtained from
CANCOPY (Canadian Copyright Licensing Agency),
1 Yonge Street, Suite 1900, Toronto, Ontario, M5E 1E5.

5 4 3 2   Printed in Canada   3 4 5/0

*To all the creative and hardworking kids
who will be using this book.*

Many thanks to my family, whose help and
support made the writing of
this book easier and more enjoyable.

The following trademarked names have been used in this book:
American Stock Exchange, Armor All, Bankette,
Bank of Montreal, Canadian Imperial Bank of Commerce,
Canadian Tire "Money," Consumer Reports, Con-Tact, Decima,
DoughNET, Dow Jones Industrial Average, Fimo, Global, ICanBuy,
Interac, MasterCard, Mondex, NASDAQ, NASDAQ Composite,
New York Stock Exchange, RocketCash, Royal Bank of Canada,
Standard & Poor's, The Dow, Tyvek, VISA, Yellow Pages, Zillions

Contents

Common Cents: **Money Basics**

Before Money

In primitive times, families and small tribes were
self-sufficient. They made or gathered or hunted
everything they needed, and needs were simple.
If a person did not have what he needed, he could
sometimes arrange a trade, goods for goods:
firewood for fish, berries for meat. This kind of
trading is known as bartering.

It was an imperfect system, to say the least. What if you needed fish, but had nothing that the fisherman wanted in exchange? Or what if he needed what you had, but you didn't need fish now — but would want some later? People wasted a lot of time just figuring out how to make good trades.

When people started keeping livestock and planting crops, about 10,000 years ago, a new system was born. People started using commodities — useful, tangible things, as opposed to ideas or services — as something to exchange with. The commodities used were always those that were understood by everyone, and that had value in themselves. They became the original currency, or money.

Grains such as barley worked well, in that they had value and were easily divided into small quantities. However, the grain spoiled easily.

On the Micronesian island of Yap, women used strings of shells as currency, but men often used large stones. Some were about 50 centimetres across, while larger ones measured up to 4 metres and were propped against the dwelling as a sign of wealth. Each stone had a hole in the centre so two men could put a pole through to carry it. Today, these huge pieces of stone are reserved for ceremonial use only, and the U.S. dollar serves for everyday commerce.

$ Cattle were also used for thousands of years by many cultures, but they didn't divide easily. Also, one result of this was that sickly cattle were kept alive. (We don't throw away paper money because it gets messy, do we?) Herds weakened from being over-crowded in pastures. Then wars were fought to get more grazing land.

Buddy, can you spare an almond? These humble nuts — as well as tobacco, beaver pelts, alcohol, drums, ivory, jade, amber, cacao beans, whales' teeth, nails, and bullets — have all served as money at one time or another.

$ Cowrie shells were a very common kind of currency, especially in China, New Guinea, and Africa, because they were valued as decorations and for their use in healing ceremonies.

$ Another commodity money that was widely used in ancient times was salt. Salt was valuable because it kept food from spoiling and greatly enhanced the flavour. It was formed into sticks or bars, 25 to 30 centimetres long and about 4 centimetres thick. These became very dark from passing from hand to hand.

The word salary, which means "regular payment," comes from the Latin word for salt allowance, salarium, because people were once paid their wages in salt.

In the early days of settling North America, a very successful form of money was *wampum*. Making wampum ("string of white shell beads") was originally an art form. The beaded ropes or belts were used by Aboriginal people for commemorating events and agreements, sending messages, making apologies, paying fines and ransoms, and as gifts and prizes. They were also used ceremonially in marriage proposals and burials. Pieces of wampum could contain thousands of clamshell beads and took many hours of labour to produce.

Once the settlers saw how much the Native people valued wampum, it evolved into a tradable commodity. The explorers began trading goods for wampum from southern tribes, and using it to buy beaver skins from northern tribes. It eventually became the official money for several of the American colonies.

This could not go on, however. For one thing, wampum was never accepted for payment of debts outside North America. People also began to make cheaper, counterfeit copies of wampum with more modern methods. Eventually this form of currency completely lost its value.

Currency is very useful in several ways. It is a medium of exchange, and that means we can buy and sell with it. It helps people to understand the value of things, including work. It also has the very handy talent of storing value. We can get currency by selling something or working for it, and keep it until we need to buy something later.

Having a system of currency helped societies become more prosperous. The ease of currency-based exchanges let people spend more time improving the quality of their goods and services. And they could easily buy the things they didn't make themselves.

Early Coins

Historians tell us that metal currencies probably began in the cities of Mesopotamia — today's Syria and Iraq — around 3500 BC. There, silver was cast into spiral and ring shapes of measured weight and value. (Commodities such as barley were still used for lesser values.) The use of measured weights of precious and non-precious metals gained steam — across the Middle East and into Greece, India, and China — over the next few thousand years.

Metal was an excellent choice for currency because it was durable and because it had real value in itself. Early metal currency systems did have their problems, though. Sometimes people cheated by using impure metals or by rigging the scales. So, to give traders confidence in the value being represented, a ruler would grant the use of his official seal on the weighing scales. This led to stamping the official seal on the money itself.

Coins have almost always featured a portrait of an important person — a ruler, for example — on what's called the obverse, or head side. The reverse, or tail side, shows some other meaningful emblem.

The first known coins were made around 640 BC in Lydia, a city on the Mediterranean in what is now Turkey. Made of electrum (a naturally-occurring mixture of gold and silver), they were fine works of art, decorated with images such as lions and bulls — emblems of well-known Lydians. Later the coins were struck in pure gold and silver, and these were very valuable. The coins brought so much wealth to one Lydian king that his name is still remembered in the saying "as rich as Croesus."

Around 600 BC, the Greeks began to make gold and silver coins. They kept the right to mint money (stamp metal into coins) for the government, and each city state had its own mint. The Greeks travelled the world with their new currency, and as their culture rubbed off on the countries they traded with, so did the kind of money they used.

The First Paper Money

Though paper money banknotes were known in China in the ninth century BC, it was not until the 1600s AD that such money was produced in Europe.

Since coins were heavy and difficult to hide from thieves, the use of paper money was a big improvement. Well-known and trusted people sometimes sent hand-signed notes certifying that the bearer of the note had deposited a certain sum of money with them. These notes would serve as promises to pay the specified amount in "real money," or coins. After a while, the notes began to circulate in the same way as coins, from person to person, without being immediately changed into coins.

*I*n the ninth century BC, a severe copper shortage put a halt to Chinese coinmaking. Luckily, China was the first home of printing and papermaking techniques, and it was able to use these to create the first paper money banknotes. The notes were made of mulberry-bark paper and were as large as napkins!

First goldsmiths (people who worked the metal) issued paper bills based on the gold stored in their vaults. Then a Swedish bank issued notes in 1661, and the Bank of England soon after that. The first French paper money was issued in 1716.

When European nations made paper money it was always backed up by gold, at first in full, and then in part. If there were ten thousand British pounds written up on paper, there were ten thousand pounds worth of gold in reserve at the bank. Now money's value is tied to people's trust in the government, rather than to actual gold.

Paper money quickly became complicated in design to make forgery more difficult. A watermark — a picture formed by thinner areas in the paper — was another identifying device. Eventually, paper money came to be made from engraved steel plates that allowed for extreme detail in the design, and banknotes became amazing works of art.

The first Canadian paper money In New France in the late 1600s, there was a severe shortage of money, especially coinage — and money was needed to make commerce possible. When a shipload of money failed to arrive from France in 1685, playing cards, specially cut and signed by the Governor of New France, were declared legal tender and used to pay the governor's soldiers. The cards were redeemed when French money became available. The playing-card money was issued until 1719, and again from 1729 to 1760, before it was officially retired.

The **Canadian** Connection

When the British took over the colonies at the end of the Seven Years' War in 1763, British money was introduced and was the official currency for almost a hundred years (although Mexican, American, and Spanish money was commonly used here, too). The first dollar banknotes issued in pre-Confederation Canada were produced by the Bank of Montreal in 1817. Meanwhile, banknotes in New Brunswick, Nova Scotia, Prince Edward Island, and Newfoundland were issued in British pounds.

In 1857, the Province of Canada decided to leave the British system of pounds, shillings, and pence, and go with the decimal system used by the United States. Other regions of what would become Canada switched to dollars and cents, too, over the next couple of decades — though their currencies weren't compatible until 1871. By that time, after Confederation, the province of Canada was issuing "dominion notes."

In the United States, the National Currency Act of 1862 served the country's growing economy by creating a national banking system. Canada simply didn't need a central bank until the Great Depression of the 1930s struck. Most communities before that time were rural and fairly isolated, so local money served just fine.

In the late 1800s in Canada, there were several corrupt-bank scandals. Take the example of the Bank of Western Canada. After it collapsed, it was found that its owner, a tavern-keeper, had been circulating false banknotes to our American neighbours.

It wasn't until the Bank of Canada Act of 1934 that an official central bank was created, and dominion notes were replaced by Bank of Canada notes. Before this, chartered banks with multiple branches were allowed to issue paper money, and the Bank of Montreal served the needs of the government.

Through the years since Canada changed over to the dollar, the Canadian dollar has been worth less than, and occasionally more than, the U.S. dollar, fluctuating back and forth. Why does it do this? It has to do

The first banknotes produced by the Bank of Canada were unilingual. Some were printed in English, and some in French.

with the demand for our dollar among investors. If demand is strong, and there isn't enough to go around, the value of the dollar goes up. If demand is weak, and there's too much going around, the value of our money goes down. This principle is called supply and demand, and it holds true for everything being exchanged. The value of each dollar in terms of the other is called the exchange rate.

Soon after the 1954 series of Canadian banknotes was issued, rumours began to fly. The notes, featuring a portrait of Queen Elizabeth II, came to be known as the "Devil's Head" series, as there appeared to be a grinning demon in Her Majesty's hair. The Bank of Canada quickly had the printing plates corrected.

The Mint

The Royal Canadian Mint, with headquarters in Ottawa and production facilities in Winnipeg, produces almost all of Canada's coins. A staff of 700 people turns out fine quality coins for circulation as well as for collectors. The Mint even makes coins for other countries.

In fact, the Mint is a great money-maker in more ways than one. It made a profit of $21.7 million in 1999. Why? Coin collectors around the world snapped up several commemorative coins honouring the new millennium. All the profits made by this Crown corporation go to the Canadian government.

The Royal Canadian Mint can produce up to 750 coins per second.

An example of a commemorative coin produced by the Mint is the $100 coin struck from 14-karat gold to celebrate the fiftieth anniversary of the province of Newfoundland. This beautiful coin featuring an iceberg, a pitcher plant, and a puffin, all symbols of Newfoundland, was released March 31, 1999.

Some of the coins that the Mint makes never circulate at all. That's because people who know their true value will keep them rather than spend them — and they cost much more than their face value (the value that appears on them). For instance, the fifty-cent coin for 2000, featuring a portrait of birds of prey, was sterling silver and sold for $19.95.

Our coins

The money we use in Canada today includes seven coins, all of which have the face of Queen Elizabeth II on one side and a Canadian symbol on the other. They are:

coin	emblem	metal	weight (g)	width (mm)	edge
One cent	maple branch	zinc core with copper plating	2.5	19.1	plain
Five cent	beaver	cupro-nickel (.75 copper; .25 nickel)	4.6	21.2	plain
Ten cent	*Bluenose II*	nickel	2.07	18.03	reeded
Twenty-five cent	caribou	nickel	5.07	23.88	reeded
Fifty cent	Canadian coat of arms	nickel	8.10	27.13	reeded
One dollar	loon	aureate bronze	7.0	26.5	plain, 11-sided
Two dollar	polar bear	metallic (nickel/aureate bronze)	7.3	28	reeded alternating with plain

Source: Royal Canadian Mint

Sometimes it happens that a banknote or coin stops being legal tender. In that case it can be exchanged for current money at a bank, but can no longer be used in normal business. For example, the British pound note was retired, and replaced by a coin, in 1984. Canada has gone the same route, replacing both the one-dollar and two-dollar bills with durable coins (in 1989 and 1996, respectively).

What's in a (nick)name?

There are many kinds of money, just as there are many cultures and languages, because long distances separated societies from one another in the past. Money developed with many looks and many names.

How does the Mint know how many coins to make? Coins are produced according to demand from financial institutions such as banks. There's little demand for the fifty-cent coin, so few are produced. Only a half-million half dollars were produced in 1999.

$ The names of coins sometimes represent the weight they originally stood for, as in the British pound or the Israeli *shekel*. Other times the name, or nickname, reflects the metal the coin was originally made from, as in the nickel or the Dutch *guilder*.

$ Sometimes the name comes from the portion of a unit the coin stands for. This is how some of our coins are nicknamed: dime comes from the Latin word for tenth, cent comes from the Latin word for hundred, and quarter needs no explanation.

$ The word dollar came from the *Joachimsthaler*, a large silver coin minted in the valley of St. Joachim, Bohemia, in 1519. The Germans shortened the name to *thaler* and the Scottish changed it to dollar. The Spanish coin worth eight *reales* came to be known as a dollar, too, and the name was adopted by the Americans for their first money.

$ Another way coins have gotten their names is from emblems they bear, such as crowns, crosses, lions, and eagles.

How coins are made

1. First blanks (coin shapes with no design) are cut from sheets of metal. The blanks are then heated in an oven to soften them.

2. Next they are washed and dried.

3. To sort out misshapen blanks, they are put through a sorter called a riddler.

4. Next a rim is raised on the edge of the blank to give it strength. The rim-making machine is called an upsetter.

5. The next step, striking, presses in the design on each side.

6. Finally, an inspection looks for imperfect coins.

What's in a (nick)name?
(Canadian edition)

$ The loon emblem almost never made it onto our dollar coin. The Royal Canadian Mint had chosen to use the same die that was used for a dollar coin in 1935. It featured a voyageur and an Aboriginal person in a canoe. But on its way to the Mint, the master die was lost! So, on June 30, 1987, the "loonie" was born. (What would we have called the voyageur coin?)

$ Before the Royal Canadian Mint introduced the new two-dollar coin on February 19, 1996, there was much discussion as to what to call it. It has a polar bear on the tail side, so lots of names had to do with the great white creature. But "toonie" — a strange name mixing its two-dollar denomination with a rhyme for loonie — has taken over.

The Bank of Canada

Unlike a regular bank, the Bank of Canada runs the country's monetary affairs — as well as designing, producing, and issuing paper currency, and guarding against its counterfeiting.

The Bank of Canada designs Canadian banknotes to be beautiful, strong, and hard to copy.

Banknotes are printed from a combination of seven engraved metal plates. Forty notes fit on each sheet of special paper, which is made up of 75 percent cotton and 25 percent wood fibres.

It's a crime

Only the Bank of Canada has the right to print Canadian money. When someone else attempts to produce money, it's called counterfeiting — and it's a crime. Through history, people have tried to make fake money, and the punishment has often been harsh. The Royal Canadian Mounted Police work together with the U.S. Secret Service and an international police force called Interpol to prevent counterfeiting.

Before recent times, counterfeiting was accomplished by engraving and printing from metal plates, very much like the ones used to print official bills. It was a long process and took a lot of skill.

Tough Bucks Imagine bills that don't get crumpled or torn, that don't get stuck in the bank machine, and that can be recycled once they're old! They do exist. Australia's banknotes are now entirely made of polymer (plastic). And money made of Tyvek, another tough synthetic, has been used in Haiti, the Isle of Man, and Costa Rica.

Did you know that it's illegal to make any kind of likeness of money, even if you don't try to pass it off as real?

However, advances in technology have made it much easier for counterfeiters. Colour photocopiers can produce reasonable copies of paper money. Computer scanners can transfer the image of a bill into digital form and then a colour printer can print a copy of a bill. These copies can usually be recognized with careful examination, but most people don't pay attention to the money they receive.

The Bank of Canada uses special techniques to make it harder for counterfeiters to make exact copies of bills. Get out your magnifying glass and check these out:

> **P**art of the cotton used in making Canadian banknotes comes from recycled blue jeans!

$ Small green discs called planchettes are added to the paper pulp for genuine bills. These can actually be lifted off the paper, leaving a round inkless space underneath. It's impossible to lift the dots on counterfeit bills because they're printed on with the rest of the picture. The planchettes also glow under ultraviolet light.

$ The printing on genuine bills is of very fine quality, the lines crisp and clear. Some of the lines, including the word Canada, are slightly raised. (These raised lines are harder to feel on older bills.) The lines on counterfeit bills often look less distinct.

$ No two genuine bills will ever have the same serial number. The serial number has three letters followed by seven numbers.

$ Each note has very fine microprinting in the background. The number that tells the value of the note is repeated in wavy lines behind the portrait. Other lines say "Bank of Canada 10 Banque du Canada 10" (or whatever the denomination, or bill value, is).

$ Newer bills have an Optical Security Device. This small, shiny patch is made up of layers that make it appear to change from gold to green.

$ The areas around the edge of a genuine note look like a plain colour, but are really covered by very fine lines running in a number of directions.

What to do if you get a fake banknote

It's rare, but it could happen. Keep the note and write down the serial number. Call the RCMP and give them the note. They'll need to know where you got it.

The Bank of Canada does not exchange counterfeit money for real banknotes, and it's a crime to pass it on to another person knowingly. So the person accepting bad money always loses out. That's why it's important to pay attention to the money you receive.

What about damaged bills?

You might be glad to hear that the Bank of Canada can help identify the value of banknotes that have been badly damaged – burned, shredded, decomposed, or contaminated. Such bills can be sent, carefully packaged, to the Bank of Canada, taken in person, or sent  through a regular bank.

The Bank of Canada will figure out what the money is worth and you'll get undamaged bills in return. If you have most of a banknote, your own bank will probably exchange it for a whole one.

Current Canadian five- and ten-dollar bills have a life expectancy of about one year. The Bank of Canada withdraws worn-out bills from circulation and just burns them in an incinerator, or has them shredded.

Shred for sale

Processing centres in Mississauga, Ontario, and Montreal, Quebec, handle the task of shredding banknotes that have been pulled from circulation. Did you know that you can actually buy this stuff? Yes, a 13-kilogram box of banknote "shred" — which looks a bit like confetti — can be yours for only seventeen dollars plus tax.

E-money: A New Kind of Cash

We use ABMs (automated banking machines) to make deposits and withdrawals, pay bills, and transfer funds from one account to another. We can bank over the phone and on-line by computer. We can buy things with a debit card, which immediately deducts the money from our bank account. Lots of people have their earnings deposited directly into their bank accounts; still others have regular bill payments automatically withdrawn. These are all examples of electronic funds transfers.

But what about cash in a smart card? With this special kind of card, users can "download" money from their account, use the card almost like cash till the funds are used up — then load it up again.

The smart card is already in use in Europe, and it's slowly making its way to our side of the ocean. From February 1997 to December 1998, Guelph, Ontario, was the site for an experiment in the use of this kind of money — known as Mondex money, after the company that developed it.

Thousands of Guelph consumers used the cards during the trial period. Hundreds of businesses accepted Mondex money. Buses and taxis were equipped with Mondex units, as were parking meters and public telephones. Funds could be loaded onto the card by phone, using special identification codes. Parents could transfer allowances from their cards to their children's. And since small card readers could be hooked up to personal phones and computers, even hot-dog vendors and babysitters could be paid with the card instead of cash.

After a while, the program started to get a bad rap from some of its users, who weren't convinced about the security and privacy of the system. So the experiment was stopped. But that's certainly not the end of the smart card in Canada. The technology is evolving, and Mondex and others are still experimenting with it. Experts predict we'll all be shopping with electronic money in the near future.

Make a
Buck!

That **All-Important Allowance**

Now that you know what money is, how can you get
your hands on some?

You can earn it yourself by providing a useful
service. You can ask your parents for money when you
need it for something special. A third way is to arrange
for a regular transfer of funds — from the people who
have the money, to you. It's called an allowance.

Why get an allowance? The advantage is that you
get paid regularly. This means that instead of asking

for money over and over and taking the chance of being turned down just when you really need something, you receive a set amount on a schedule. Does that mean you'll have money whenever you need it? Not necessarily. You'll probably always think you need a little more than you have, no matter what. But you do get the chance to manage your own money, and try to make it cover what you want the most.

A 1997 survey conducted by Global/Decima found that, on the average, Canadian ten-year-olds earned seven dollars a week in allowance. Fifteen-year-olds' allowances averaged fifteen dollars.

Different families have different ways of handling allowances. Figuring out what's best for you and your family will take some discussion. Typically, allowances are doled out once a week or once a month. Every week works best for most kids: if you get a big chunk once a month, you'll have to avoid the temptation to blow it all at once. Some parents like to pay their kids on the day they get paid themselves, or when they get cash from the bank for the weekend, for example. Some experts suggest making Sunday allowance day, so all the money doesn't get spent on the weekend. You might want to mark allowance day on the family calendar to help everyone remember.

Some kids pay no attention to the way they spend their allowances. For many, however, an allowance is a chance to practise good money-management skills. Kids sometimes set aside an amount from each allowance for higher education, for a big purchase, or simply for the sake of getting into the habit. Other kids give regularly to worthy causes — another good habit to get into.

Your side of the deal

Some allowances are free of strings. The kid gets the money just for being a part of the family. Other kids have a list of chores they have to do to earn the allowance. If you have a set list of chores, you might make a chart to help you keep track of the different daily and weekly jobs. Check them off when they're done.

There are some jobs that are so time-consuming or complicated that many parents would pay someone else to do them. Why not be that someone else yourself? Cleaning the garage (ask before throwing something out!), washing the windows, beating the carpets, and trimming the rose bushes (gloves!) might fall into this category.

The key is always to negotiate with the folks — you might as well learn this useful skill now. Work out together how much a certain job might be worth to them, and then try to do a good job. You might get paid more if you offer to do an especially good job, like waxing a floor after washing it.

Here are some of the chores commonly done by kids:

Pet care – feeding and walking, sometimes grooming and poop pick-up

Kitchen – setting the table, clearing the table, washing and/or drying the dishes

General clean-up – vacuuming, sweeping, taking out the garbage

Own bedroom – clean-up, bed making

Yard work – mowing, raking, watering, snow shovelling

The big question: how much?

Allowances vary from kid to kid, of course. Some are big enough to cover all the kid necessities: transportation, meals at school, clothing. Kids who get these big allowances have a lot more responsibility to make sure that their money is spent wisely. Other kids get only enough to cover the extras: snacks, CDs, movie tickets. Sometimes parents and kids work out a special separate allowance, such as a clothing allowance. Families should agree from the beginning on just what the allowance is to cover, so everyone has the same understanding.

In general, kids get more money as they get older and (hopefully) better able to handle it. How wealthy a family is doesn't always affect the size of the allowance. It depends more on how the parents feel about kids and money. But for some families, the budget can manage only a very small allowance, or none at all. (If this is your life, read on for great ways to earn money.)

Some parents decide on the amount of allowance by looking at "the cost of living." You can help yours figure this out by making up a list of your typical weekly expenses, and adding up the dollar amounts for them. They might be surprised at how much things cost compared to when they were kids!

Your folks might be influenced by knowing how much allowance your friends get, but don't nag or be too pushy. The bottom line is to talk and be reasonable.

Why did everything cost a nickel in the good old days?

Inflation is what makes things get more expensive year by year. So what is it, exactly? Most experts refer to it as "too much money chasing too few goods." When there's more money going around, prices rise. Inflation goes hand in hand with a healthy, growing economy. Luckily, when the cost of living goes up, up, up, most people make more money, too. So things aren't harder to buy, just higher priced.

*I*f you thought kids could receive allowance only as cash, you might be surprised to hear that some families have a different system. Instead of giving the kids money in hand, some parents run a banking system, keeping records in a book or chart. Each allowance payment is added to the running total and kids "withdraw" cash from the parent-bank as needed.

The up side is that the money isn't lying around in danger of getting lost, and the kid might think more carefully about purchases and so save more money. But the down side is that the parent might not have the cash on hand when the kid wants it, and might be a bit more controlling about how it's spent.

The World of Work

Getting an allowance is one way of making money. Doing extra chores around the house can sometimes boost your income. But chances are good you want a little more cash than those sources will provide. You might be ready to earn some money on your own.

But first, think about yourself as an employed or self-employed person. Can you be responsible and reliable, keeping your appointments on time? Can you deliver your product or service with quality and a polite manner? Can you do the work even if your friends are tempting you to slack off and go to a movie? Can you budget your time wisely?

Take a good look at your schedule. How busy are you right now? Attending school takes up a lot of your time. Add homework, special projects, extracurricular activities and clubs, helping out at home — and what's left? It might help to actually map out your activities on a chart or calendar and see the big picture. Maybe weekends are the only time you can spare. You might decide you can really work only in the summer.

You also have to consider how far away prospective jobs might be and how you can get to them. Are they close enough to walk or ride your bike to? Is there public transportation that can take you there? You'll need to consider what it might cost you to get back and forth to your work. That will cut into whatever money you make.

One very important thing to think about is job safety. You should never do a job that you think could be hazardous. Make sure the job you choose is suitable for a kid. Your parents can help you decide.

And finally, don't forget to keep your life balanced. It would be useless for you to spend so much time making money that you neglect your schoolwork, ruin your health, or totally give up the joys of fun and friendship. (But you knew that!)

You can be glad that in Canada today, school is considered the primary job of kids. Child labour laws prevent the exploitation of children in work settings. Only a hundred years ago, little kids would be sent up chimneys to loosen the soot for removal, or made to spend long hours selling on the street.

What are your interests?

Have you ever heard the popular saying, "Do what you love and the money will follow"? It's good advice for anyone. When you like what you're doing, it almost doesn't seem like work. You can turn some of your favourite activities into money makers.

So, what are your interests? Are you an animal lover? Do you like little kids? Do you like to cook? To be outdoors? Are you artistic? Musical? A computer whiz? Take this quick quiz to find out more about your work likes and dislikes:

1. Where are you most comfortable spending long hours?

a) In a climate-controlled room

b) In the great outdoors

2. Are you happier in groups or alone?

a) I love to be part of a winning team.

b) I prefer solo challenges.

3. How much routine can you handle?

a) I like to know what to expect from my day.

b) I'm happiest when things are constantly changing.

4. How outgoing are you?

a) It takes some time for me to warm up to new people.

b) I like to be the life of the party.

5. Are you a self-starter?

a) I prefer it when someone gives me a plan to stick to.

b) I like to come up with new ideas and make them happen.

6. How do you feel about little kids?

a) Love 'em!

b) They're sweet — from a distance.

7. How handy are you?

a) I'm all thumbs.

b) I'm pretty good at making things from scratch.

ANSWERS

1. If you picked a), don't get a job planting trees – you're probably shy of the elements (you know, rain, hot sun, dirt). And if you picked b), you might not feel at home in an office. Being comfortable where you work is more important than you'd think.

2. Entrepreneur types usually pick b). If you wind up doing all the work in group school projects yourself, and *loving* it, you'll probably do just fine starting your own business. But if you picked a), make sure you find a work environment full of people to cooperate with.

3. If you answered b), forget that factory job. Try for a job that lets you do new things, or at least see new faces, every day. If you picked a), you probably have no problem with routine jobs, because you can find ways to pass the time – by gabbing with a co-worker, for example.

4. If you picked a), avoid sales work, which demands you be comfortable talking to lots of people. Choosing b) means you like an audience, and can make small talk with anyone. Try sales, or even entertainment!

5. If you chose a), you might be best suited to a very structured job. If you don't mind following strict orders, there are lots of jobs like this, usually with bigger, well organized companies. But if you picked b), and can handle the risk of failure, you'll probably be better off starting your own empire.

6. Did you answer b)? Most kids automatically turn to babysitting when they need to earn some extra money. But think it over first to make sure this kind of work is right for you. You really need to love little kids to do a good job. If you chose a), you're probably a natural.

7. Had trouble answering this one? Be honest. If you've sewn your own Halloween costumes since you were six, or your room is full of models you designed yourself, you have a built-in money-making skill — pick a). But if all the craft projects you've ever started are still half finished, that might be telling you something . . .

More questions you can ask yourself:
- Is there something that you've always wanted to do?
- Is there something that people say you're good at?
- Do any of your friends do work you think you'd enjoy?
- What do you really like doing?

Different types of work, same area of interest . . .

Say you like plants and gardening. If you want to work for someone else and get paid regularly and reliably, you might try for a job with a local nursery. There are many jobs to do in that area. You can seed, make cuttings for rooting, water, clean up the greenhouses, arrange stock, or help customers.

If you prefer to work for yourself and provide a service, you can do yard work or gardening for people in your neighbourhood.

If you prefer to make something to sell, you might raise new plants from seeds or cuttings and plant them in decorated pots, to sell door to door or at craft sales and bazaars. Are some good ideas coming to mind?

Working for your parents

For some kids, this is a great solution: you get a lot of experience without all the stress of working for someone you barely know. As long as you get along well, working for your folks can be great — for a while. But before you drop everything and join the family business, make sure it's the right type of work for you. The kind of work that makes your parents beam with pride might not do much for you.

Lending a hand

Why would you want to do volunteer work? There are lots of reasons. For one thing, it might be for a cause that you believe in and can contribute to. For another, the experience you get in your volunteer job might be just what you need to prepare you for a paying job in the future. You might meet nice people and make some new friends, as well. And it's less boring than just hanging out.

Out in the community, there are fundraisers like car washes and door-to-door selling for a good cause. Public libraries sometimes need volunteers, as do hospitals, seniors' residences, and animal shelters. The "volunteers wanted" section of your community paper lists all kinds of opportunities.

There are even things you can do at school. You can lend a hand in the library: shelving, putting the cards back in returned books (if the system isn't computerized), and helping younger kids find what they need. Some schools even let reliable students ring the bells and answer the office phone during lunch hour. Maybe they need monitors to keep the sports equipment rounded up or someone to raise and lower the flag. If your school has a garden or aquarium, you might be needed there. You can be a reading buddy or tutor to a younger student. You can work on the school newspaper or yearbook.

Once you start looking, you'll find all kinds of places where your skills can be put to use.

The experience you get can be really helpful. It can show you what it means to have someone counting on you to do a good job.

Get a job

So you've decided that you'd like to try working for an employer. What do you need to know?

There are minimum age restrictions on many kinds of jobs. In Ontario, for example, construction and logging workers must be at least sixteen years old. The minimum age for factory jobs is fifteen and for workplaces other than factories, it's fourteen. (Age restriction rules don't apply if you're working for your mom or dad.) As well, fourteen- and fifteen-year-olds can't work during school hours unless they've been officially excused under the terms of a special regulation.

Make sure you know the age restrictions in your area, and find out the current minimum hourly wage for students, too. It's your right to make that much.

If you don't already have a social insurance number, you'll need one. This is the number by which the government keeps track of your earnings, taxes, and other matters. You can apply for your SIN at a Human Resources Centre of Canada office. The one in your area will be listed in the blue pages' Government of Canada listings, under Employment and Insurance.

What's tax?

Nothing drives people crazy like tax — it's money that goes to the government. And it's illegal not to pay. Tax money covers the government's expenses and helps to pay for programs and services like health care and education. These are two of the most dreaded taxes:

Sales tax is added to the cost of many of the things we buy. It's the GST (goods and services tax) and PST (provincial sales tax), or, in some provinces, the HST (harmonized sales tax). We pay this tax at the cash register when we make our purchases.

Income tax is a percentage charged on the money that a person makes. By the end of April every year, the government makes sure that all working people officially report how much they've earned, and that all income tax is paid up in full. That explains why your parents look so frazzled every spring.

Getting hired

Almost everyone looking for a job makes what is called a resumé. It's simply a summary of you, your talents, and your work history.

It takes a while to build up the experience that can make an impressive resumé, and as a kid you might not have much to start with. (That's why volunteer work can be so valuable.) So you'll need to create a "picture" of yourself as a person by listing your hobbies, interests, and any organizations you belong to. A character reference (a letter saying that you're honest, hard-working, etc.) from someone reliable can help give an employer confidence. A school guidance counsellor can help you make up your resumé, and many books can help, too.

While you're looking for a job, let people know what you're looking for, just in case they hear of something. Family and friends can help you make connections. Check the job ads in newspapers' classified sections, too. Small community papers can be an especially good bet for hunting down decent kid jobs.

Don't be shy! If there's a company you'd really like to work for, give them a call and ask for a chance to visit and talk about possible job opportunities. There might be a small job there that would be just right for a kid who's eager to learn. Whatever your interest is, follow it. Read up on it, attend amateurs' club meetings, and talk to people who do the kind of job you want to do. Whether you want to work in radio, with horses, or with small airplanes, you can find people to network with, and who can help you learn more about the field.

What about income tax?

In Canada, there's something called a "personal amount," which is the biggest amount a person can earn without having to pay income tax. Most kids don't make more than that amount, and in most cases don't even have to file an income tax return. (That is, send an annual statement of earnings to the Canada Customs and Revenue Agency, like your parents do at tax time every year.)

The personal amount has been in the $6000 range for some time, but it's subject to change, so you'll need to look up the Canada Customs and Revenue Agency in the blue pages of your phone book, or on the Internet, for up-to-date info.

Before you're eighteen, employers generally won't subtract income tax payments from your paycheque. But if income tax is "withheld," you'll have to file an income tax return to get the money back, as an income tax refund.

If you apply for a job and are called for an interview, be sure to arrive on time and suitably dressed. Try to know something about the company before you go. Be polite and positive. A good attitude is a great selling point!

How to read your pay stub

That important piece of paper, your paycheque, is finally in your hands. But wait — there isn't as much here as you'd been expecting! And what's this bit of paper attached to it? What are all these subtractions?

The pay stub explains exactly how much you made altogether (it's called your gross pay), for which period of time — as well as what kind of deductions have been made. Here's the math:

Gross pay

- **EI** stands for Employment Insurance. Workers who pay into this government program are eligible for a period of financial assistance if they're let go from a job, as well as for maternity, parental, and sickness benefits.
- **Income tax** may come off your paycheque regularly, too.
- **Union dues** are paid by some workers in exchange for membership to a group that works for their rights.
- **CPP** stands for Canada Pension Plan. This is a program that all working Canadians over age 18 pay into. (Except that Quebeckers have the QPP instead.) The money is pooled to provide a small retirement income to people aged 65 and up. (If you're under 18, this shouldn't be deducted from your pay.)

= **Net pay**

Breaking it off

If you get fired, don't get angry right away. Find out from your employer what was lacking in your performance. Listen politely, and respond politely if you have something to say. You don't want to make enemies or "burn your bridges."

Sometimes employers have to make staff cuts. The decision often has more to do with who's newest than with who's doing a poor job. Laid-off workers often get rehired when times get better for their companies.

If you think you were unfairly fired, you might need to take action. But be sure to talk it over with your parents and think it through carefully before you do anything.

If you need to quit your job, be sure to let your boss know well ahead of the time you plan to leave so he or she can find a replacement. Two weeks is standard, but in some cases you might want to give even more notice. Remember, happy employers are more likely to give you glowing references down the road.

Going solo

If you're working for yourself, you will earn money by selling something. That something might be a product, like lemonade, or it might be a service, like babysitting. You'll need to decide what product or service to provide, whether there is any demand for it (or whether you can create a demand), and how much to charge for it. You'll be wearing many hats — all of them, in fact, if you work alone. So you could consider teaming up with a partner. You might find someone with different talents from yours, so that the two of you could complement each other.

As you plan, don't forget that every kind of business has pressures. If you decide to make a product to sell, you might find yourself with a large order to fill by a deadline. If you're providing a service, you'll have to be available when the customer needs you.

The ins and outs of running a business

At King George Senior Public School in Guelph, Ontario, a group of students and a teacher set up a classroom tuck shop, so they could sell snacks to their fellow students at lunch break. Student volunteers took turns handling the many tasks involved in running the shop. They learned to use a cash register, weigh out bulk candy, make change, keep track of inventory (the stuff they were selling), order more from wholesale suppliers when needed, and keep track of income and expenses on the computer. They even dabbled in advertising and planned special sales events. Some students were involved in training other students.

This was great job training. But the kids also learned what it takes to run a business — which will come in handy if they decide to try it themselves one day.

What steps would you need to take to start and run your own business? Here are some suggestions.

Get ready, get set

Many entrepreneurs try to focus their aims on paper before they launch their business. A business plan doesn't have to be complicated. It states what product or service will be provided. It also says who the buyers will be, and how they will be attracted, or what the competing businesses are, and how they will be dealt with. Market research can help you answer these questions. Call local business organizations, read competitors' ads, and talk to family, friends, and potential customers.

Another thing to do is to test your service or product, and make sure it's a worthwhile one. If you're offering a service, practise doing it to make sure you're really good at it. You might need to do some studying to improve your skills. If you're creating a product, make up a sample to see if it works and how long it takes to make. Show it to a few people whose opinions you trust, and ask what they like about it and what improvements they might suggest. (Try to ask people who aren't family, for a more impartial opinion.)

Pricing is very important. If the price is too high, no one will buy. If it's too low, you won't make enough to stay in business. Examine your competitors' products. Are yours as good? Better? What are their prices like? Businesses starting out sometimes try to price their products in the middle range of what's being charged.

You should also try to estimate your profit margin. That's the difference between your costs and your selling price. Will there be enough profit to allow you a decent wage for your work? These may be just projections (predictions), but they will help to prepare you for what might happen.

And finally, you'll need some start-up cash. That's money for buying supplies, creating advertising, or just making change.

Drumming up business

Sometimes customers just fall into your lap, but more commonly, you have to find them. Advertising can make people aware of the product or services you're offering.

Business cards might sound very official, but they can be printed up pretty inexpensively at a business supply store or copy centre, or you can make up a few yourself on a computer. You can also create brightly coloured flyers that state what you're selling and how to get hold of you. (Ask your parents before listing your phone number or address!) Use interesting fonts to create a logo, or add some clip-art graphics for extra appeal.

It's better not to quote your price on a flyer or business card, for several reasons. You might decide to change the price, up or down, as you gain more experience. Also, you might have reason to offer different rates to different customers.

Of course, you'll want to put these advertisements where they are most likely to be seen by your kind of customer. Where would you find people who need babysitting? How about a daycare centre, or a pediatrician's office? People needing pet care might be reached at the vet's office, the pet-food store, or a popular dog park. Supermarkets and community centres often have bulletin boards that can be used for ads.

A way to reach lots of people without having to walk too far is by putting flyers under windshield wipers in parking lots. (You'll go through tons of flyers, though.) Ask your local government if this is allowed before you do it. And be very careful not to damage any cars.

Going door to door with flyers — assuming you've talked it over with your parents first and they think it's okay — works well if you want to concentrate your work close to home. You can even ring the bell and personally ask people if they're interested in what you are selling. Giving a good impression of yourself — with a positive attitude, polished look, and a smile — can make people more inclined to buy or hire. Offer one of your flyers so they can call you later.

Some businesses will allow posters for upcoming events to be placed in their windows, and might allow small-business ads. For example, if you want to do custom knitting, get friendly with the manager of a knitting-supply store. Show him or her the quality of your work, and you might be allowed to place an ad in the store. Your ad will benefit both you *and* the store's customers, who might be looking for your service.

It might also be worth the expense to advertise in a local newspaper's classified section. Small neighbourhood papers are cheaper, and they still reach a large readership. Even better, if you can think of something unique about your business, you might drum up some free publicity by getting written up in the paper.

Many businesses these days are on the Internet. Internet service providers often include space for a personal Web site in the cost of the connection. If your business hopes to reach beyond your own neighbourhood, and you can deliver a product or service by mail or over the Internet, then this is the obvious way to advertise. One young Canadian entrepreneur founded his own Web site design company and attracted clients from far and wide. They loved his work — and didn't realize he was only eleven years old!

Don't forget that word of mouth can be one of the most effective kinds of advertising. Your family and friends can be very helpful just by talking up your business and perhaps handing out your business cards. Satisfied customers can also help to spread the word.

Customer service

- It goes without saying that you should put your best foot forward with your customers. Be polite, appropriately dressed, and well groomed.
- You also have to be reliable. That means be on time, do the job the way you agreed to do it, and be honest and responsible.
- Some jobs require more promptness than others — the very obvious one being babysitting. The lawn might be able to wait, but a parent who needs to get somewhere often can't.
- If you're unable to show up for a job, call well in advance to explain why and apologize. Arrange a make-up date and make sure you're there on time.

- When working in people's homes, take extra care to show them that you're trustworthy. A letter from a respected adult vouching for your honesty and reliability will make clients feel secure.
- Be very respectful of your employers' privacy. Don't look at their private belongings or repeat things you've overheard (unless it's a matter of safety).
- Of course, don't take or use anything without permission, and eat only what you've been invited to eat.
- You also need to look after yourself and not do anything that puts you at risk. If a person or situation makes you feel unsafe, leave the house or yard.

Handling payments

It's important that you be at ease handling your customers' money. They're used to polished, professional service from stores and other businesses, and they'll expect you to count out change in a way that's easy for them to follow.

Let's say you've just sold something for seventy-five cents, and the customer hands you a dollar. Count back the change out loud, so the customer can hear you clearly. Start with the amount it costs ("So that's seventy-five cents..."), then hand over, say, a nickel ("...eighty..."), then a dime ("...ninety..."), then another dime ("...one dollar."). How would you count change for a twenty-dollar bill if the sale were $15.45? Practise making change over and over until it comes very naturally. This will inspire confidence in your customers.

Another good habit is to give customers a receipt for the amount they've paid. Make two copies — one for the customer and one for yourself. (Having a copy yourself helps you keep track of the money you take in.) Business supply stores sell carbon-sheet receipt pads, so you only have to write once. Or you can make up your own receipt forms on the computer, including your name, the name of your business, and your contact information. This will give the customer a way to reach you for future business.

Here's a sample receipt:

Pamper-Pup Dog Walking Service
Jamey Johnson
102 Parker St.
Winnipeg, MB
555-2444

Received from ....

The amount of ....

For ....

Date ....

Signed ....

If you get a cheque for your work, look it over carefully. Amazingly, sometimes people forget to sign cheques, or they fill in the wrong date. Make sure the amount is correct, too. It's easier to get people to fix a mistake when they're standing right there.

Buying supplies

When it comes to supplying your business, it really pays to be a careful shopper. If you need to buy large amounts of one item, you might be lucky enough to qualify for a wholesale discount. Check the Yellow Pages for wholesalers, and call and ask. Also look at discount stores and wholesale clubs (if you know someone who has a membership). Sometimes catalogues or on-line stores can be good sources of unusual materials. Some projects can even be done with second-hand or scrap supplies that can be obtained cheaply or free.

Keeping records

An essential part of a successful business is accurate record keeping. Don't rely on your memory! After every sale, write down the product or service that was delivered, the date, who paid for it, how much was paid or is still owing, what form of payment was received (cash or cheque), and any comments that might be important later. (The customer will be impressed if you remember special details, though you should get new instructions each time if you're not sure.) You can keep everything in a computer file, notebook, or box of index cards.

Keeping financial records is very important. You'll need to know what running your business is costing you before you can figure out how much you are making. Remember to include the cost of supplies, advertising materials, and transportation expenses like bus fare.

• •

Keeping records is the only way to find out if you're making a profit. If you're creating a product, add up the cost of your supplies and divide by the number of products you can make from them, to see how much each one is costing you. Also, keep track of how long it takes you to make each one. If you make several at once, divide the amount of time it takes by the number of products you make. You might be able to speed up production as you gain practice.

• •

BUSINESS COSTS — Jade's Homemade T-Shirts

SUPPLIES

12-pack plain white T-shirts	$40
fabric paint	$20
TOTAL for 12 T-shirts	$60 (each $5)

LABOUR

my salary	$5 per hour
time to decorate 12 T-shirts	6 hours
TOTAL for 12 T-shirts	$30 (each $2.50)

TOTAL COSTS	$7.50 each T-shirt

$10.00 selling price
− $ 7.50 costs
$ 2.50 profit per T-shirt

Taking stock

After your business has been running for a while, look at how things are going. Have you been able to make a profit? Do customers seem happy with your product or service? Have you had any repeat customers? Are you enjoying the work?

If things are going well, you might even decide to enlarge the business — seeking out more clients, or expanding into other areas. If you've been selling snacks in summer, you might continue with a menu of cold-weather treats. If

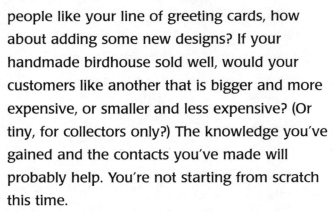

people like your line of greeting cards, how about adding some new designs? If your handmade birdhouse sold well, would your customers like another that is bigger and more expensive, or smaller and less expensive? (Or tiny, for collectors only?) The knowledge you've gained and the contacts you've made will probably help. You're not starting from scratch this time.

Even if your first business didn't go well, the experience you gained was probably worth the work you put into it. Everything you do helps you learn the ropes — even the mistakes you make.

Great
Money-Making
Ideas

You've taken a good look at yourself and what you like to do. You think you have what it takes to be a good worker. You've settled on several areas of interest, but would like to see some real examples of good jobs for kids. Check out these ideas!

Delivery and distribution

Leg power gets this job done. You might deliver flyers to homes or businesses, or place them on car windshields. You might attach posters to utility poles or city walls and fences, if that's permitted where you live. Phone books also need to be delivered to houses and apartments each year. At election time, candidates might hire you to distribute election signs for lawns. The standard kid job, of course, is the paper route.

Garage/yard sales

In our society, people love to gather — and get rid of — clutter. You can take advantage of this with a garage sale. Choose a date (weekends are best), and put out signs around the neighbourhood and perhaps in a newspaper. Gather goods to sell (your own stuff, or stuff your parents or friends just want to get rid of any way they can), and make them look as good as possible. Invite friends to bring things to sell for themselves. Think about making extra money selling snacks. Make price tags or stickers. (Visit some other garage sales ahead of time to see how things are commonly priced.) Set up a few tables for displaying goods. A place to hang clothes on hangers is nice. Be ready really early — people show up way before they're supposed to. Have a container to hold money and lots of change on hand. And be willing to haggle a bit over prices. That's part of the fun.

Bake sale/refreshment stand

Everyone loves home baking. With permission from your school, you can try selling baked goods to teachers at recess, to students at lunch or recess, at special performance nights or parents' nights at school, or at school fairs. Other markets for snacks are community  events such as literary or music festivals. (You might need a licence to sell in public places. Ask your local goverment's permits department.) Your uncle's Christmas-tree farm or the ice rink can be a great place to sell hot chocolate and baked goodies. Popular parks, the swimming pool, and hiking trails can also be good. A booth at a local farmer's market is a place to establish a regular clientele. You can even sell from a stand in your front yard.

Make something popular like brownies, or specialize in something different. Popcorn is cheap and it can be made in different flavours for extra appeal. Wrap each serving individually in plastic wrap; a little ribbon tied on it looks nice. You'll need to invest in disposable cups and plates or napkins, and should also have garbage and recycling containers. Keep your table clean and attractive. Flowers in a little vase are a nice touch. Remember a cash box and lots of change.

Plants

If you're patient and careful, you can turn inexpensive seeds into beautiful plants. Talk to some gardeners for good advice. They can help you choose plants that do well in your area.

Some really easy projects: Squash seeds are big and sprout quickly — and many people don't want to be bothered growing their own for just a few plants. Zinnias are an easy-to-plant flower that comes in lots of colours. Seedlings sell well, but if you have enough land for growing, you can take some plants to maturity and then sell the vegetables. Tiny tomatoes are delicious and grow in great numbers in a small area with the proper care.

Little expandable peat pellets are convenient and clean for starting plants. Buying in larger numbers will get you a better price. If you buy plastic divided containers, you'll have to mix or buy potting soil. An old window can make the top of a little greenhouse (called a cold frame), with some boards for sides. Or if you have a friend with a true greenhouse, maybe you could use just a little area on one of the benches for your project. Artificial plant lights make a big difference in the early months of spring. They're a pretty big investment in the beginning, but will last for many years.

Car washing

If you love cars, taking special care with them can get you repeat business. Cars should be washed in a shady spot. Hose off the excess dirt, then sponge on the soapy water, starting at the top and working down, one side at a time. Don't forget the tires. Rinse and dry the car with a chamois or soft towel.

If you do inside cleaning as well, you'll need a vacuum and an outside electrical outlet, or a grounded (three-pronged, for safety) extension cord. Hand vacuums are easy to use, but don't clean as well as the full-sized ones. The car owners can probably provide theirs to use. Suck up the loose dirt, and then clean and polish the car inside with a product like Armor All. Take the mats out and wash them if they're dirty, then let them dry and replace them. Remember to polish the windows and mirrors, too.

Greeting cards

Greeting cards and gift tags are always popular and can be made in many different ways. You can use computer graphics programs, paint them with watercolours, or decorate them with dried flowers (see below). Black ink drawings reproduce well by photocopier — add a few watercolour touches or leave them plain. Hand-printed cards are easy to make and photocopy. Even potato prints can be great on cards.

Your own photographs can also decorate greeting cards. Having multiple copies made of a single print brings the price down. Choose a paper colour that will enhance the photo and cut it to fit a standard envelope.

Dried flower projects

The designs of nature can be very appealing. Dried flowers pressed flat and covered with clear Con-Tact paper or rice paper make lovely decorations to hang on the wall. You can dry your own flowers between sheets of paper towel and heavy books. Flowers with thin petals and no really thick parts work best. (Make sure you don't pick too many of one kind in any area or the flowers won't be able to reproduce.) If you prefer, and can afford to buy them, pressed dried flowers can be ordered from catalogues and over the Internet. Leaves, ferns, and grasses work equally well.

Use dried flowers to decorate homemade candles, lampshades, and the fronts of photo albums. Dried flowers can also be placed between glass and the glass sealed with metallic stained-glass tape (you'll need an adult to help). You can glue dried flowers onto wood surfaces like furniture or trays and cover them with many coats of decoupage coating. Another cool thing to do with flowers is to scan them on a colour computer scanner. Just lay the flowers out, cover and scan. Then you can print pretty images to frame or use on stationery, without using up lots of flowers.

Fancy lettering

Although computers can now produce amazing fonts of every size with the touch of a button, there's still a certain charm in hand lettering with ink on elegant paper. Fancy decorative  lettering is called calligraphy. This lettering requires special pens and special know-how. You can take a course or learn by studying a book. You'll need a steady hand and lots of practice. Mistakes will be hard to correct, so extra care is needed to get it all right. Use calligraphy to make certificates, decorative pieces to hang (nice combined with an illustration), fancy invitations, or menus.

More craft ideas

Christmas ornaments sell well for a few months every year.

If you knit, try mittens. They're small and fast and kids are always needing more after losing them. If you're a beginner, scarves are simpler. You can even use up scraps of yarn by adding nice stripes!

Handmade jewellery is popular — especially things made with beads or sculpted from Fimo, found at craft stores. You can make your own craft dough more cheaply; check the library for recipes.

Decorated ponytail holders (scrunchies) are expensive to buy at stores, but easy to make.

Painted clay flower pots are popular, too. You can also try making things out of clay yourself. Some towns have specialty shops where you can paint and fire clay items.

Try selling your creations during special events at school — especially at holiday concerts — to parents, friends, and teachers.

Craft fairs will bring your customers to you, but you'll probably have to pay for table space. Display your crafts nicely and have them clearly marked with price tags.

If Mom or Dad wears one of your creations to work, there might be orders from co-workers!

Birdhouses and feeders

Can you use a saw, hammer, and nails? With help
from an adult, you can make birdhouses and
feeders from cheap or even free scraps of wood.

There are specific kinds of houses for different
birds. The size and shape of the house, the size of the hole,
whether or not there's a perch, whether it sits on a pole or
hangs – these are all important details that you'll need to
check out. Local wildlife associations and birding clubs can
direct you to the right set of plans.

Button making

Buttons are easy to make – and people like to wear them
to support a team, state an opinion, or advertise a special
event. Button makers are expensive, starting at around $60
for a beginner's model, but can pay for themselves pretty
quickly. You can also buy a gadget to help cut the circles.
Each button requires parts, such as a base and a backing with
a pin, and these are cheaper if bought in larger numbers. Since
buttons are sold for two to three dollars, there's a good profit
to be made.

Child care

You might like to take care of young children –
when the parents are away, or just busy at home
doing something else. Take your job seriously
and take a babysitting course. Learn safety rules.
Get important information from the parents. Learn how little
kids act and what they like to do. Take a few puppets over to
do plays with. Keep a collection of children's books to read to

the kids, or pick up some at the library. You could also take a tape of nice kids' music for them to listen to. You'll be asked to work a lot if the kids enjoy their time with you.

Entertainment services

Can you clown or do magic tricks? You could find yourself in demand at birthday parties and local fairs. You might even put on a puppet show with puppets you make or buy, and a script you have written or adapted from an old standard like a fairy tale. What about running storytelling sessions for kids in your neighbourhood, charging a small fee? Use your dramatic flair to make the characters come alive. (Practise on your friends.) Props and costumes add extra punch to your act. You could also develop a skill, like making balloon animals.

Animal care

If you like animals, walking dogs and visiting cats can seem like playtime. Most pets need attention regularly. They need food and companionship. Cages need to be kept clean. Learn about animal care and you can be in big demand. Get detailed instructions from the owners and keep the phone number of their vet handy. You might also find work sitting small animals in your own home.

House cleaning

Do you hate cleaning your room? Strangely enough, you might not mind cleaning someone else's house. Of course, as with any job that takes you into someone's home, you must be careful with clients' belongings and respectful of their privacy. Be sure to use only cleaning products that the client approves or supplies, and never throw anything away unless you're *sure* it's garbage.

Coaching/tutoring

What are you really good at? Math? Baseball? You can help younger kids learn something they're having trouble with. Patience is very important so that your client doesn't get discouraged. (Remember how it felt when you were just beginning.) Make sure you know your subject very well. Ask advice, if you need to, from experts in the field. Then give it your best.

Running errands

There are probably plenty of people in your neighbourhood who are unable to get out and around and who would benefit greatly from your help. For busy people, having someone to drop off and pick up things can be a real time saver. Your time can make your money!

Birthday-party planning

Some parents are so busy that a party planner can be a lifesaver. If you do parties often, you'll learn from experience and it will get easier. You'll learn just where to go for decorations and loot bag items and maybe get a discount for buying in quantity. You can provide the snacks or even a simple meal. You can arrange for entertainment and get to know what little kids enjoy most. Your entertainment list can include clowns, magicians, and musicians. You can provide materials and instruction for crafts or games. It's a nice idea to offer parents a choice of activities, so the party can be tailored to the child. Plan around a theme, like "space," "the rain forest," or "at the beach."

Does this sound like a job for more than one person? Two or more partners working together is a good plan. Want less responsibility? Advertise as a party helper. Busy parents can use help even if they've done the planning themselves.

Computer support

If you are very good at working out simple or even more complex computer problems, you can probably

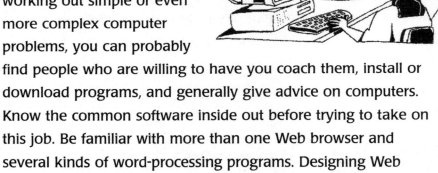

find people who are willing to have you coach them, install or download programs, and generally give advice on computers. Know the common software inside out before trying to take on this job. Be familiar with more than one Web browser and several kinds of word-processing programs. Designing Web pages is another possibility. Kids are making a huge impact on the computer world!

Muscle work

Are you into working up a sweat? There's a lot of muscle work to be done out there. Offer your services for yard work in all seasons. There's mowing, raking, weeding, pruning (with the owners' exact instructions), preparing gardens for planting, brush hauling, snow shovelling, and small pond cleaning (gloriously sloppy). Window washing, driveway sweeping, and garage clean-up are other suggestions. These jobs don't require much in the way of skill — just hard, careful work. Never do anything you consider dangerous. Discuss with your parents what's appropriate for you.

Office/clerical work

All kinds of work fits under this category. Office work can include filing, organizing, photocopying, answering phones, typing, running errands, making coffee, watering plants — even going for doughnuts. Some jobs, like addressing and stuffing envelopes, can be done at home. With word-processing software, you can maintain mailing lists and produce mailing labels for companies. If you're a fast typist, you can key in handwritten essays and term papers on the computer.

Keeping Tabs on Your Money

Saving for a Rainy Day

Why save? Why not just spend now? First, if you have some money set aside, you'll be ready for anything.

Let's say you want to start your own business. If you've been saving money all along, you might just find you have enough start-up money in the bank. Then you won't have to go looking for someone to lend you the money.

Or let's say something goes wrong, like you hit someone's car with your skateboard. You might have the money in the bank to repair the damage, instead of having to ask your parents to pay for it and owing them money.

Maybe you just want to have enough money stashed away that you can grab that great deal at the mall.

Then, of course, there is your future. Higher education costs a bundle — and you might be the one who's going to have to pay for it. You could always get a student loan, but with the interest added on these are expensive and take a long time to pay back. Why not put some money aside now that can help you later?

The secret of saving is to spend less than you make and stick the extra away. It's easiest if you just decide on an amount you want to save, and put it away regularly, without question. You could even have your parents divide your allowance into saving and spending money. Or you can keep a savings account and take money out only for special needs.

Bank on It!

What was your first bank? Where did you put your pennies to keep them safe? A jar? A purse or wallet? Maybe you had — or still have — the classic piggy bank. That's fine for a bit of money, but what if it starts to overflow? And what if you want your money to do more for you than just sit on a shelf? Then the time has come for you to use a real bank.

But first, what is a bank? A bank is an organization that borrows and lends money, and that most people rely on to hold their money. There are advantages to using a bank. Your money is safe there. You won't misplace it, and nobody will borrow it to pay the paper carrier. If the bank is robbed, you'll still have your money — guaranteed.

In some kinds of accounts, the bank will pay you for the privilege of having your money. That payment is called interest, and it's a certain percentage of what they're holding for you.

How can the bank afford to pay interest? Because it uses its customers' money to make investments, which bring in a big profit. Banks lend money to other banks (sometimes just overnight!). The bank also gives loans to people and charges them a higher rate of interest than it pays out.

Having your money in a bank can be convenient. You can withdraw your money from any branch of your bank across Canada, even though you deposited it at your home branch. You can go directly to a teller in the bank or access your money through an automated banking machine (ABM) at the bank or many other places. You can write a cheque or make a direct payment with a bank card, instead of carrying cash. And you can cash cheques that are made out to you.

It's all about interest

As you now know, interest is the fee the bank pays for holding people's money — as well as charges people for borrowing its money. How does it work? Let's say you have $100 in an account that pays 3 percent interest for a whole year. Three percent of 100 is three, and that's how many dollars of interest you'll earn. So you'll end up with $103 at the end of the year. That's if the bank is paying simple interest, calculated just once at the end of the year. In the real world, most banks calculate and add the interest on a daily or monthly basis, so the interest then earns interest itself. This is called compound interest. With larger amounts of money and over longer periods of time, even a small difference in interest can make a big difference to a bank account.

Borrowing money

When people need more money than they have at the moment — to make a big purchase, or to cover school fees, for example — they can take out a loan. Banks, and other institutions like trust companies, lend people money for an agreed-upon length of time, and charge them interest on it.

Doing the math for simple interest is . . . well, simple. Just start with the principal — that's the amount of money being borrowed or lent. Multiply the principal by the percentage and you'll have, in dollars, the amount of interest to be paid. If the loan goes past a year, then you can multiply by the number of years, too. Borrowing $100 at 8 percent for one year, with simple interest, will cost you eight dollars. For two years, the interest will be two times eight dollars, or sixteen dollars.

Compound interest is trickier to calculate. Banks have computers that do the math. There are also charts in books, and interest calculators on the Internet, that are easy to use.

Most adults owe money to a bank, usually in the form of a mortgage. (Have you ever noticed your parents getting stressed at the mention of this word?) A mortgage is the kind of loan people take out in order to buy a house. And it's usually the biggest amount of money a person ever has to borrow. Mortgages often take decades to pay off, especially when the compound interest is factored in. Banks also offer a loan arrangement called a line of credit. With this plan, the money — up to a certain limit — is always available, and interest is paid only on the money used.

Taking out a loan is like signing a contract. People who fail to follow carefully the payback schedule get a bad credit rating (like a bad reputation), and might not be able to borrow money in the future.

Your bank account

Choosing a bank

For kids, convenience is probably the number-one reason to choose one bank over another. How close a bank is to your home, and the hours it keeps, will probably help you choose. You might want to use the same bank your parents do — that way they can put your account on their bank cards, and transfer money to you electronically.

Service fees can take a chunk out of your money, so watch out for these. Most Canadian banks offer special youth service plans for people up to age eighteen or nineteen. You can often get a special no-fee account that includes many or all of the banking privileges that adults have, including chequing and ABM transactions. Since these plans change over time, it is best to ask for up-to-date details from the banks you're interested in.

Opening an account

If you decide to open an account at a bank, you'll need to take a parent or guardian in with you. Be sure, too, to bring at least two pieces of signed identification and your social insurance card. The bank will want a copy of your signature to keep on hand in case there's ever any doubt about who's

> **U**sed by about a third of Canadians, credit unions are cooperative financial institutions, owned and run by their members. The members usually have something in common — like the place they work, or their cultural background. Credit unions are most popular in Saskatchewan, British Columbia, and Quebec (where they're known as *caisses populaires*). They offer most major banking services.

signing your cheques. If you want to start off by putting in some money, take along some cash or a cheque made out to you. (You don't need to deposit money right away, though.)

If you open a chequing account, you'll be given some starter cheques, and asked to order and pay for a personalized chequebook, which will be mailed to you later.

Keeping score

Once your money is safely socked away in an account, you'll no longer be able to dump out your life savings onto your bed and count it whenever you please. So how do you figure out how much you've got in there?

There are several ways for you to keep records of your banking — it'll depend on your

What kind of account?

If you don't plan to take out money often, the **savings account** may be a good bet. In this type of account, you can take out your money at any time, but you can't write cheques on it. Savings accounts usually pay more interest than chequing and combination accounts.

A **chequing account** is one that lets you store your money as well as take out money from an ABM, make direct payments, and write cheques. These accounts don't always pay interest, and if they do it's usually a fairly low rate.

There are also **combination accounts** that let you earn a bit of interest, while also having money handy.

Talk it over with someone at the bank to find out which type of account is best for you.

bank and on the type of account you have. Youth accounts commonly use a passbook, a small booklet that is updated by the teller (or at some ABMs) each time you deposit (put in) or withdraw (take out) money. If you ever forget your passbook, the teller will give you a receipt and the transaction will show up the next time you have the book updated. (Get in the habit of checking the figures to make sure they're correct. Mistakes can happen.)

If you have a chequing account, you'll get a booklet called a register to write all your records in. Each time you write a cheque, make sure you record it. Write down the name of the person or business you've written the cheque to, the date, the cheque number (it's in the upper right-hand corner) and, of course, the amount of the cheque. Also, write in all the deposits you make to your account.

The last step is to figure out your balance: that's the amount you currently have in your account. You just subtract, from the previous balance, the amount of each cheque you've written — and add the amount of each deposit you make. If you always subtract each cheque you write, you'll know how much you've promised and what you have left to use.

Some bank accounts send out monthly account statements instead of using a passbook. If you have a chequing account, along with your statement you may get back any cheques you've written that have been processed (these are called cancelled cheques). Mark these in your register by putting a tick in the box next to the cheque description. This is important! If you keep track now of which cheques have "gone through" and which haven't, then you won't get any nasty surprises later.

Cheque It Out

If you're using a bank, chances are you're using cheques. Even though there are all kinds of newer ways to pay for things, cheques — legal promises to pay — are still popular with most Canadians. They're convenient. You can send them in the mail, and you can write them as you need to without having to carry money around. And they're safer than cash.

If your bank account lets you write cheques, you'll have a book of cheques printed with your name and address, the name of your bank, and your account number. Here's what else goes on a cheque:

How to write a cheque

1. Grab a pen. It's got to be in ink — ballpoint is best because it won't run.

2. Write the date at the top.

3. Write the name of the person or organization after "Pay to the order of".

4. Just to the right of that, write the amount of the cheque in numerals.

5. On the line below, spell out the dollar amount in words, and put the cents in numerals over the little "100" on the right. (If there's any space left after you write in the dollar amount, draw a line through it so no one can turn your $4 cheque into $400,000.)

6. The line marked "memo" lets you add a word or two of information, for record keeping.

7. Last but not least, sign the cheque — but only after you make sure that all the information is correct. (If you make a small mistake, you can cross it out and put your initials next to it. If you make a big mistake, write "void" in big letters across the cheque and start a new one. Don't forget to mark the same thing in your register.)

Rubber cheques Bouncing a cheque is writing a cheque when you don't have enough money in the account to cover it. This would become an NSF (not sufficient funds) cheque, and would be returned to the bank of the person you gave it to. That promise of payment you made when you wrote the cheque? Broken.

You can understand why anyone who gets a rubber cheque from you (bounced — get it?) might not want to do business with you again. Also, banks usually charge a penalty for bouncing a cheque. And businesses that receive bad cheques can also charge penalties.

If you write a cheque and decide later that you don't want the money taken from your account, you can ask the bank to stop payment on the cheque. Of course, you need a very good reason to do this — a mistake, loss, or theft, for example. And the bank will charge a fee for this.

Taking it to the bank

When a cheque is made out to you, you can cash it and get the money in hand, or you can deposit the amount into your own account. In either case, sign your name and write your account number on the back of the cheque. That's called endorsing the cheque. If you're banking it, it's a good idea to also write "For deposit only." Don't sign the back until you're about to cash or deposit it, though — once a cheque is endorsed it's as good as cash and could be lost or stolen.

You can also sign the cheque over to someone else by writing "Pay to the order of [person's name]" before signing it. Then that person can take the cheque to his or her bank.

It's important to know that the money from a cheque you deposit might not be ready to use from the moment you put it in. The bank needs to check the cheque writer's account to make sure there's enough money there to cover it. That could take several days, or even much longer if it's a cheque from a foreign country. If you deposit with a teller, ask if there is any hold on the funds. If you're using an ABM and have any doubts, ask a bank employee.

Other types of cheques
you can get at the bank

Traveller's cheques are a safe way to carry around money when you're outside of the country, because they can be replaced if they're lost or stolen. They're accepted in many places like cash. (Lots of people prefer to withdraw small amounts at a time from ABMs instead, since these can now be found nearly everywhere in the world.)

Money orders and certified cheques are promises to pay that are guaranteed by the bank. You pay for a money order, and the bank prints it up — for the exact amount, and with the name of the person you're giving it to. A certified cheque is written by you and stamped by the teller. The money is then withdrawn directly from your account, so the cheque is guaranteed not to bounce. Mail-order businesses often require these guaranteed kinds of cheques.

So Many Ways
to Bank

In person

Before lining up to see a bank teller, you first have to fill out a special transaction slip with your name, account number, and the amount you want to deposit or withdraw. You can use a deposit slip from your own chequebook which shows your name and account number, or you can get a slip from the bank counter and enter the information yourself.

Deposit slips have spaces for listing cheques and cash separately, in case you're depositing both. If you're depositing only cheques but want to take out some cash at the same time, there's a place for writing that in, too. If you're withdrawing cash, you'll need to sign the slip while the teller watches.

	CURRENCY	20.00
March 15 ___ 200 1 ___	COIN	.75
Devin Watson	CHEQUES OR COUPONS (List on reverse if necessary)	30.00
DEPOSITED BY		
Devin Watson	TOTAL	50.75
(Please sign here in presence of teller)	LESS Received in Cash	5.00
	AMOUNT OF DEPOSIT $	45.75

The Canadian Imperial Bank of Commerce launched Canada's first cash dispenser in 1969, and the Royal Bank of Canada followed a few years later with its "Bankette." (The world's first was installed in June 1967, in Enfield, U.K.) Back then, the machines were often known as "robot tellers."

At an ABM

If you have a transaction card for the bank
machine, your card's magnetic strip will tell the
machine who you are and what accounts you
have with the bank. So you don't need to make
out a transaction slip. The bank machine records,
processes, and stores your information and the
transaction. To make sure that no one but you
uses your card, the machine asks you for a PIN, or
personal identification number. (You choose your
PIN at the bank when you're given your card.)

The convenient thing about bank machines is
that they're available twenty-four hours a day. But
it's safer to use the machines during the day than
at night. And remember, if a bank machine
location feels unsafe to you, don't use it.

Stay on the ball

- Never write down your PIN any place where someone could
  find it, and keep it separate from your bank card. (Better yet,
  don't write it down at all — memorize it. And keep it to
  yourself.)

- Don't choose an easy-to-guess PIN, like your birthday or
  street address.

- While you're keying in your PIN, shield the keypad with
  your hand so no one can watch.

- Take your money, bank card, and transaction slip from the
  machine, and tuck them into your wallet right away.

It's also a good idea to . . .

- Keep your bank card in a plastic protector to keep the magnetic strip in good shape. If it gets damaged, your card might not work in the machine.

- Hold onto your transaction slips to check against your bank statement.

Phone and on-line banking

For people who have to pay lots of bills and juggle different accounts, banking by phone or on-line is great. But you can't make deposits or withdrawals this way, so most kids don't have much need for it yet. If your parents have your account set up under their phone or on-line banking password, they might let you use it to check your balance, keep an eye on your transactions, and find out which cheques have been cleared. No line-ups – and fewer fees, too.

You can be sure that electronic banking will become a big part of your life as your banking needs get more and more complicated.

Grow It!
All About
Investing

What Is Investing?

Investing is making a commitment with your money, in the hopes that it will grow into a bigger amount. Yes, your money can actually earn money. And if you invest when you're young and leave your investment to grow, the results can be astonishing.

Through the magic of compound interest, you can see your money double and redouble itself over time.

Want to know how long it will take to double your money? Use the Rule of 72 to find out. Simply divide the number 72 by the interest you'll be making, and the result will be the number of years it will take. (This trick also works in reverse: divide 72 by the years, and you'll get the rate of interest.)

at **2%**, your money will double in **36 years**
at **5%**, your money will double in **15 years**
at **10%**, your money will double in **7.2 years**

So, the interest rate makes a lot of difference. If you keep adding money to your savings when you can, then what you add will start to grow, too, making more money for you.

What is risk? It's the possibility of something going wrong. When you invest your money, you risk losing some or all of it. Some investments are riskier than others — and sometimes it's the riskier investments that pay off the most. The stock market is definitely risky, though some stocks are considered to be safer than others.

RRSP season: what's all the fuss about?

Many Canadians invest through a government program called the Registered Retirement Savings Plan (RRSP). The RRSP has two special features.

First, the money that's put in — which is limited to a percentage of what a person makes — can be invested tax free. That means that the part of your income that's put into an RRSP doesn't have to be taxed right now. It is taxed when it's withdrawn, which is usually once you retire from work. Since retired people generally have less income, they pay a smaller amount of tax on the savings.

Second, the interest that the money earns while it's in the RRSP is not taxed, so there's more interest building up and earning more interest. The earlier in your working life that you start saving in an RRSP, the better. A few years can make a huge difference in the amount of compound interest that heaps up.

There's an annual deadline (at the end of February) for buying RRSPs, if you want to get the income tax relief for the previous year. And lots of people wait until the last minute to buy them. So that's what RRSP season is all about — lots of advertising, and lots of late hours kept at the bank and other financial institutions.

The Registered Education Savings Plan (RESP) is a Government of Canada program that encourages parents to save for their kids' post-secondary education. Contributions made by parents, grandparents, or even non-family are helped along with government contributions. The money grows tax-free until you begin to use it to pay for your higher education. You, the student, then pay tax on the money — but at a low rate, or not at all.

Types of Investment

Term deposits and GICs

These are safe and simple — though you won't make big bucks with them.

Savings accounts always have a lower rate of interest than other investments, because the bank can't count on you leaving your money with them. You can take it out whenever you want. But you can earn a little more interest if you promise to leave the money with them for a certain length of time — that's a term deposit. The money you invest in a term deposit can be withdrawn at any time — but you will pay a penalty. A similar investment is the Guaranteed Investment Certificate, or GIC, which is "locked in," so you can't get your money out until it matures (reaches the end of its term).

When a term deposit or GIC matures, you get your money back along with all the earned interest. Usually, the longer you invest, the higher the interest rate you can get. But since interest rates go up and down all the time, the main risk with a term deposit is that your money might be locked in at a lower interest rate — while the rates are going up.

One little hassle is that kids can't own stock (or mutual funds or bonds other than Canada Savings Bonds) directly. Your parents can set up a trust account for you in their names, however.

Bonds

When you buy a bond, you're lending money to someone who promises to pay you back, with interest. The interest and the maturity date of the bond are set when you buy it. So it's a bit like a term deposit, only it doesn't come from the bank, and it does pay a higher rate of interest.

Bonds are issued by the federal government (Canada Savings Bonds), by the provinces (provincial bonds), by cities (municipal bonds), companies (corporate bonds), and by foreign countries (international bonds). Bonds issued by reliable governments are considered to be safer than corporate bonds because a company is more likely to go bankrupt (broke) than a country. Bonds are given ratings according to how risky they are — from AAA to D, right on down to "junk." The really risky bonds offer the highest interest rates in order to get people to buy them. You've been warned!

Canada Savings Bonds (CSBs) are very safe and popular — especially as gifts to kids. They're sold at banks, credit unions, trust companies, and brokerage companies, and through payroll savings plans at work. The bonds come in numbered series and are sold for a limited period of time, called a campaign, which lasts about six months each year.

CSBs come in two types. Regular interest bonds ("R" bonds) hand over the interest annually. Compound interest bonds ("C" bonds) reinvest the interest, so the investment continues to grow until the bond matures or is cashed in. CSBs can be redeemed at any time, but must be in place for at least three months in order to earn any interest. There are also Canada Premium bonds — they're similar to CSBs but can't be redeemed until a full year after the purchase date.

The interest rates for each new CSB series are announced and advertised in October, before sales begin.

For more information on other types of bonds, financial advisors at brokerage firms and banks can help.

Stocks

Do your parents watch the financial news on TV, or read the business section of the newspaper? Does it all seem like so much gobbledegook? You're not alone. Here's some basic information that will help you understand the world of stocks.

Stocks are shares of a company or corporation. When you buy shares of a company, you own a part of it. Shareholders get to read the company's annual financial report and can voice opinions and vote on issues at annual general meetings.

How do you actually make money on the stock market? People shopping for shares try to buy good stock at a low price. Then, if prices get higher, they can sell their shares and make back more money than they spent. That extra money earned is called a capital gain. As well, some companies pay dividends (a portion of their earnings) to their shareholders. In this way, shareholders can make money without having to sell.

Shares are traded (bought and sold) at a stock market, or stock exchange. In Canada, we have stock exchanges in Toronto, Montreal, Alberta, Vancouver, and Winnipeg. Some of the bigger U.S. markets are the American Stock Exchange, the New York Stock Exchange, and the NASDAQ. The NASDAQ is unique because it's an electronic market (on-line instead of in an actual building). This exchange includes many high-tech companies and handles a very high volume of trades.

Each exchange lists many companies, big and small. Companies have to apply to get listed, and they have to follow lots of rules and regulations once they're there.

What's a Dow? Unlike the prices of the things you buy in stores, stock prices go up and down like crazy all day long. These price changes are called fluctuations.

Watching fluctuations helps some people get a sense of the big picture — that is, how healthy our economy is. The ups and downs are measured out on a kind of scale called a stock market index.

The oldest and most famous stock market index is the Dow Jones Industrial Average, usually just called The Dow. The Dow keeps watch on a set of thirty important companies listed on the New York Stock Exchange, and averages out their performance every day. Some indexes, like the Standard & Poor's 500, measure hundreds of companies, and others, like the NASDAQ Composite Index, break things down into different types of industry, like transportation or telecommunications.

The Initial Public Offering (IPO)

When a company goes from being privately owned to offering some of itself for sale to the public, this is called "going public." Why do companies decide to sell shares? Because it can be a great way for them to raise money — especially if they're considered to be a "hot" business and lots of people want to invest in them.

The stock market as a whole rises and falls according to the general state of the economy, interest rates, reports by stock analysts, and local or international events such as war and weather. The price of a company's shares also says a lot about how much faith people have in the company, and in its potential for growth and profit. It doesn't necessarily reflect the real value of the company. Hot properties like Internet businesses and biotechnology companies are good examples of stocks that trade high because they're expected to make lots of money in the future — even if they aren't now.

When a company's share prices get so high that sales start to slow down, the company sometimes splits its stock — for example, breaking each share into two pieces worth half the amount. The value stays the same for the people who already own shares, but now more people can afford to buy the stock. Pretty smart!

When the confidence of buyers goes down, the price of a stock can fall very quickly, too. That's why stock buying is risky. There's never any price guarantee from day to day. Lots of money can be made and lost in a short time. So careful investors study the financial situation of a company before choosing stocks.

Some investors like to "buy and hold" — meaning they choose a company they believe in, and own the stock for a long time. Other people try to "time the market" — buying when the price is low and selling when the price rises, minutes or days or weeks later. Each investor has to decide how much risk he or she is willing to take, and which investment style is most suitable for him or her.

Let's say you wanted to invest in a stock. How would you decide what to buy? Some people like to buy shares in companies whose products they use and like. Others lean toward companies that are environmentally friendly. Still others prefer to go with reliable old "blue chip" companies, which are usually very stable.

A great way to get a feel for investing in stocks is to "invest" a fictional dollar amount in a certain stock and watch to see how it performs. Lots of schools get their students involved in this kind of make-believe investing, and there are some excellent stock market simulation games on the Internet.

To follow a stock's ups and downs, you'll need to know how to read stock quotation

"Blue chip" means of high quality or value. Why? Some people say that it's because blue gambling chips were traditionally the most expensive ones.

tables — you know, all that tiny print in the business section of the newspaper.

Down the first column are the stock symbols, or abbreviated names. Across the tops of the tables are some pretty mysterious words. Here's what it all means.

Div stands for dividend. The amount listed is what the company currently pays per year, per share.

52 week high and low indicates the highest and lowest share price the stock reached in the last year.

Yield tells you the dividend divided by the share price — a percentage figure that shows investors the return on their investment, in terms of dividend.

Some tables also give the **P/E (price/earnings) ratio** — that's the price of the share divided by the company's earnings, over the last year. Many people judge the quality of a company by its P/E — the lower, the better.

High and **Low** tell the day's highest and lowest selling prices.

Last is the closing price — the price of the last share sold at the end of the day.

The **Change** column tells you how much the stock is up (with a plus sign) or down (with a minus sign) from the previous day's closing price.

Bulls and Bears Have you ever heard of a bull market? No, it's not beef for sale! The name refers to a market that's experiencing a lot of growth. Bullish investors are optimistic types, who trade in the hopes that stock prices will continue to rise. A bear market is one in which stock prices are falling. Bearish types make their trades believing that the market is in a downturn.

There are several ways to buy stocks. Some people hire a financial advisor from a brokerage firm to help them choose and plan a whole set of investments (called a portfolio). In return for this expert advice, the firm charges a fee. There are also discount brokerage companies that offer less advice but also charge less money. Investors can even make trades over the Internet through an on-line brokerage company. This is even less expensive.

But to really save on brokerage fees — and to be able to invest in small amounts — there's one more really good, kid-friendly way to buy stock: DRIPs.

Many companies are willing to sell small amounts of their own stock without charging any fees, through a DRIP — a dividend reinvestment plan. Here's how it works: you own a share or shares in the company, and any dividends you earn are automatically used to buy more shares. You can also add money to your account whenever you choose, and that money will go to buy more shares.

You usually need to own a least one share of a company's stock to be able to start a DRIP. You can buy one share through a broker and then deal directly with the company. Or, some companies will let you buy directly from them, through a direct stock plan (or DSP) — though they might charge a fee for each purchase. There's much information on the Web about DRIPs and DSPs. Check out some financial Web sites, or use a search engine to dig up the latest.

Be careful out there

It's the same story in every business. People who sell things — investments included — are out to make money. Not all of them are honest. Investors can be misled into buying worthless stock, spending too much on a stock or paying too high a fee.

The safest way to buy stock is through an established broker with an honest reputation. Investors need to know their stuff, too. Reading companies' annual reports and keeping up with business news helps people to make good buying decisions.

Mutual funds

Mutual funds are a way for one person to make many different types of investments without having to spend megabucks. Set up and run by financial institutions, mutual funds pool the money of thousands of investors. All that money is looked after by a mutual fund manager, who shops around and makes investments in stocks, bonds, real estate — you name it. Some of the investments might do really well, and some of them might crash and burn. But in the long term, mutual funds are supposed to make money at a decent rate. A lot of people are more comfortable buying mutual funds than investing on their own, because they feel the fund manager can make better judgments.

Of course, there are fees. Some funds require a fee to get in — these are front-end load funds. Back-end load funds take a percentage of what you make when you sell your shares. (To be competitive, some companies offer no-load funds.) The company running the fund also takes a percentage each year to pay its expenses. That fee can eat up earnings by something like 2 or 3 percent.

There are some kinds of mutual funds that charge less for management fees, because they need less management. One is an index fund. This kind of fund owns shares in every stock found on one of the major stock indexes, like the Dow Jones or the NASDAQ Composite Index. Then the gains and losses of that fund will be almost exactly the same as those reported for the index itself. There's no need for the fund manager to buy and sell and run up big fees, because the list of stocks on the index hardly ever changes.

Money market funds are another kind of mutual fund. These invest in things like government notes, bills, and bonds. Money market funds are considered safe, and they're very liquid — which means you can sell them easily if you need the money for something else. They're not locked in like term deposits, for example.

Just because you're a kid doesn't mean that you can't start learning now about the world of finance. When it comes to investing, you have an advantage that older people don't have, and that's time. If you start now — even in a very small way — to put away some savings, you can grow a nice little nest egg. Other young people are doing it. You can too!

What will you do with the money you grow? Well, that's up to you . . .

The **Savvy Spender**

If I Had a **Million Dollars**...

How you handle your money says a lot about you and your goals. Does some of your money settle down into a cozy little nest of savings? Or does it just flow through your fingers, never to be seen again? Do you fall for every new trend, or do you think about how valuable something might be in the long term? Have you ever gone on a buying binge, then felt rotten about it later?

Imagine how you'd feel if you could spend less, but get more from your money! It can happen. You can have a positive effect on your spending habits, just by thinking things out and by planning. It's easy. Just ask yourself, the next time you feel money burning a hole in your pocket: do I really need this?

Before you pull out your cash or debit card, decide whether the purchase you're making is really necessary. Being a careful shopper doesn't mean you can't have fun. It does mean that when something really good comes along, you might have enough money left over to buy it — instead of always being broke.

It's the business of businesses to sell, and they do a good job of making us want what they've got. Have you noticed that celebrities are paid to do product endorsements? Does that make it a good product? Ads try to make you think you'll be happier and more popular with the product they push. The ad usually shows irresistible scenery, great-looking people, and cool music — to make you want to join in the fun. Some ads even mislead viewers about how good a product is, or what it can be expected to do. Think twice before you fall for the pitch.

Your Best Bud: **The Budget**

Put simply, a budget is a money forecast for a certain length of time, like a week or a month. You predict how much money will come in and how much will go out, and write it all out on paper. Then you hold on to the paper, and compare your predictions with what really happens.

"Budget" is a scary word for some people. It sounds rigid and strict, like something a parent might force on a kid. But it doesn't have to be that way. Used properly, a budget will help you keep track of your expenses, plan your buying, and show you the truth about your spending habits.

> *The* word "budget" comes from the French word for the little money bag carried by merchants in the Middle Ages — the *bougette.*

Ready to try it? You'll want to break down your budget into different spending categories — ones that fit your own personality. If you need to have money for some just plain goofy purchases, put in a category called "mad money." The other categories can cover more serious or long-term needs. Are you responsible for regular expenses like school lunches or bus fare? Better put that right at the top, under "Necessities." Do you like having your own money for those clothes your parents would never buy? Put it in. Does the hobby you love need a share of the money? That's a category. Do you love snacks? Maybe that needs to be included. How about a category called "Savings"? You can even have more than one, if you want to work toward several goals. Should you include a category for sharing what you have with others? Think about it.

Once you've worked out your categories, you need to figure out how much money each one needs over the course of an average week. Think about it, and try to be honest with yourself. Now add up the numbers. You might be surprised to find that on your first try, you come up with a grand total that's way more than your actual income can cover.

So you'll have to look at your categories again, and figure out which costs could be reduced. Bus fare doesn't change, so that's a set cost — unless you're close enough to walk when there's time. Could you make your own lunch at home to save some money?

Does your money go far enough? Is there anything left for savings? Donations to your favourite cause? You'll probably want to play around with your budget until it feels right to you.

Here's a sample budget for a kid who supports a hamster and a comic book collection.

MY WEEKLY BUDGET

Expenses		Income	
Bus fare	$5	Allowance	$15
Snacks	$2	Regular babysitting	
Entertainment	$5	job	$10
Pet supplies	$2		
Gifts	$2		
Comic books	$3		
Savings	$5		
Charity	$1		
TOTAL	$25	TOTAL	$25

This girl has budgeted for twenty-five dollars worth of expenses, with twenty-five dollars worth of income. She keeps cash on hand for bus fare, entertainment, and snacks and keeps money in a savings account for the other categories. She keeps written records for each category, so she'll know how much of the money in her account is to be used for each kind of spending.

So instead of giving a buck to charity every week, she keeps track of the category till she's up to ten dollars, then donates it and starts over. She has twelve dollars earmarked for comic books, so she'll have it ready when a collector's edition comes out. Right now there's ten dollars in the gift category, but that'll grow to fourteen by the time she needs it for her brother's birthday gift. She feels good about putting five dollars each week into savings.

There's no law that says you can't borrow from another category to buy something in a category that's running short. Just make yourself a note to pay it back – and remember not to take money from where it's absolutely needed.

Your budget helps you answer the question, "Can I buy that now?" It's about making decisions. And it's good training for what you'll be doing for the rest of your life.

Sharing

While you're thinking about good ways to spend your money, why not consider sharing some of it with people who really need it? Giving to worthy causes is like sharing your good fortune with others. There are many ways to share. You can put cash in collection boxes for recognized charities. You can budget in a regular amount, save it up, and mail a cheque to the group you think needs it most. (You can also help charities get more money by fundraising or donating used items.) Don't worry if you can only give in a small way. Remember, if everyone shared a little, it could make a big difference.

Pay Attention, and
You Can Save

If your money isn't going far enough to cover all your expenses, there are two solutions. One is to find more income. Go back to chapter two for some ideas on getting some paying jobs around the house or on your own. But if you've already done that and are still short, you need to get spending smart. If you can find a way to pay less for what you want, you'll have more money left over for other things.

How can you pay less?

Sometimes just by waiting a while, you can find incredible deals. Remember finding that awesome sweater on sale for half price (you know, the one you blew five allowances on four months earlier)? Weren't you fuming? You'd be pretty proud, though, if you'd waited out the season and managed to get the deal. If you have a lot of patience, and can handle the risk of missing out on something (the sweater sells out before sales season, for example), you can get double for your money. You just have to decide if you can wait. And don't forget that if you miss that sweater, you might end up with something you like even better.

Sales seasons are a golden opportunity. Try to think ahead, when you see bathing suits at

70 percent off in September. You probably won't need one for a while, but by the time June rolls around your old one might not fit anymore. You'll be glad you got a good deal now, instead of having to pay full price in June! And pay attention to quickie sales. Those jeans might be 25 percent off at the Back to School sale, but full price the next week.

> **I**mportant hint: Don't buy something just because it's on sale if it isn't what you would have liked at the full price. It won't turn out to be a good buy if you never use it.

Are you stuck on expensive name brands? Do you crave clothes covered with logos? You're not always getting better quality for your money. Are those running shoes really worth two, three, or four times more than the rest? Careful shoppers can find trendy clothes at decent prices. Look in less upscale stores (discount stores can be great), and take the time to examine clothes carefully to find the really well-made stuff.

Don't forget that not everything has to be brand new. How about checking out the second-hand music store for that new CD you want? Remember, someone else might have ditched it just a week after it came out.

Recycled clothing stores are great places to find cheap clothes that express what you're all about. You could even think about setting up a swap with a bunch of friends. Trade your too-narrow shoes for a shirt that doesn't match anything else your friend owns, and you've both got a deal.

Are you eating yourself out of your allowance? Fast food outlets and vending machines can really burn a hole in your pocket. A simple drink in a restaurant can set you back three dollars with tax and tip. Keep track of your food spending and you'll see how quickly it adds up. To really save money, pack a lunch!

How about yard sales, rummage sales, and flea markets? People sometimes get rid of stuff they just don't use — it can still be in good shape and cheap. Look the stuff over carefully in case it's broken, and don't buy unless you need it or are pretty sure you can resell it and make money.

Do you ever pay unneeded service charges? The answer might be yes if you withdraw little amounts of money at a time from the ABM, instead of keeping a bit of cash at home for expenses. Do you use other banks' ABMs? You pay pretty big service charges for that. Think about what else you could spend the money on!

Summer is a dangerous time for overspending. Kids have lots of time on their hands, and businesses have plans for separating them from their money. Amusement parks, concerts, and movies — and the snacks sold there — can take a massive chunk out of a kid's budget. Cash-smart kids ask around about a movie before sinking their cash into a ticket. They can also think of cool things to do that aren't so expensive, like bike riding, hiking, swimming, sports, and just hanging out with friends.

One last tip about being a clever consumer: read some of the consumer magazines that test and rate products, before spending your hard-earned money on something big. One magazine just for kids is *Zillions*, from Consumer Reports. You can also find product-rating sites on the Web.

Tipping

Lots of people are in the dark about tipping, but it's pretty simple: tips are like a thank you for a job well done. People who serve customers often make low wages because their bosses assume they'll get tips. The usual amount to tip for decent service is 15 percent. That goes for the person who cuts your hair, brings you food at a restaurant, or drives you in a taxi cab. There's a quick and easy way to calculate 15 percent. Take the amount of your bill, and move the decimal point one place to the left to get 10 percent.

Divide that in half to get 5 percent. Add those two figures together, and that's 15 percent. (Tippers in Ontario restaurants can get the 15 percent by adding together the 7 percent GST and the 8 percent PST.) If you didn't like the service, feel free to tip less. And if you were really impressed (and can afford it), why not reward the server with a little extra?

Canadian Tire "Money" — a form of store coupon, not currency — is printed on banknote paper and has many of the same security features as real cash. But instead of a portrait of the Queen, these bills feature everyone's favourite Scotsman, Sandy McTire.

At the store

Shopping can be so much fun — especially if you've been saving up for something you really want. But don't let the excitement of the moment keep you from being a careful shopper. Here are some things to think about.

You've already compared prices and are getting the best deal you can find, right? Are you watching as the price is rung into the cash register? Is the total, after tax, what you expected to pay? If the item was on sale, did you get the sale price?

Think about how much money you hand the cashier. Count your change. After you get your receipt, look it over to make sure it's correct. You'll be glad you developed in-your-head math skills the day you realize you've been overcharged by accident. If you can correct a mistake right at the cash, it's better than waiting till later. It saves you a trip — and everyone's memory is better right then.

Keep those receipts

Do you let those little sales slips get lost in the shopping bag? They can be worth a lot in some cases. If you discover a hole in that new shirt, you'll want to go back to the store. But if you don't have the receipt (and especially if a fair bit of time has passed), you could be out of luck. Have a special place for keeping receipts. You should especially keep the owner's manuals and receipts for big purchases that come with warranties. If there's a warranty card to mail off, remember to mail it. Being on top of this kind of stuff could mean free repairs the next time something breaks down.

When you do need to return something for replacement or repair, take along the receipt and anything else it came with. Even the original packaging and price tags can be helpful.

Most stores want to stand by their good reputations and will try to make you, the customer, happy. So there's a chance you might be able to return or exchange something even without the receipt, but it might be harder. Return policies are often posted for shoppers to see. Always be polite and honest when you're dealing with store employees. If you feel you're not being treated fairly, ask to speak to the manager.

Paying with **Plastic**

Debit card

Now as widely used as cash, Interac direct payment is a Canadian debit card service that allows you to pay without cash or cheques. Unlike the credit card system, with debit cards you can spend only money that's already in your bank account. If the money isn't there, the purchase won't be approved and you won't get the goods. That way you don't have to worry too much about overspending. And unlike with cheques, you always know when the money is actually being taken out of your account – because it happens pretty much immediately.

Sounds like a good way to shop, doesn't it? But there are some drawbacks. It's hard to keep track of debit card spending, so you still might spend more than you want to. A good habit to get into is to record each debit as if it were a cheque. You might also get hit with direct payment fees, unless your bank account has a no-fee service plan.

A recent survey found that 59 percent of Toronto kids aged nine to fourteen had bank accounts, and 17 percent used bank cards.

And security is a serious issue. Follow the bank machine safety tips on page 78 whenever you make a direct payment. Don't forget that all someone needs in order to get at your money is the card and your PIN, so make sure your PIN is a complete mystery to everyone but you. Some banks won't cover your losses if your PIN is ridiculously easy to guess.

Credit card

Though you can't get a credit card of your own till you're an adult, you're never too young to learn how to use one.

A bank just for kids Thought credit cards were strictly for adults? The Young Americans Bank in Denver, Colorado, is the only bank in the world created just for kids. It even has a credit card program for kids twelve and up. The bank promotes responsible credit card use — its philosophy is that kids who start young learn better money management skills.

Some parents make their kids authorized users of their credit cards. The kid's name appears on the card, but Mom and Dad get the bill every month.

Credit card buying is like taking out a loan. When you pay with a credit card, the credit card company pays the store. Then, once a month, they send you a bill listing all of your credit card purchases. So you can actually buy stuff when you have no money, knowing (or hoping) that you'll have the money when the bill comes in. Lots of people get in over their heads with credit card bills and take years to get out of debt. You don't *have* to pay off the entire amount each month, but if you don't, you'll wind up paying a very high rate of interest.

There are many different credit cards out there. The major ones (VISA and MasterCard) are offered mainly through banks. Others are merchant cards that can be used for purchases from those companies only. Gasoline companies and department stores usually offer these. There are also charge cards that require you pay your entire bill each month, or pay some pretty heavy penalties.

New kid on the block: the stored value card This new kind of card works something like a credit card for teens, except that parents load it up with a cash value ahead of time. Then, every month, they get a statement telling them where, when, and how much was spent.

Choosing a credit card takes some shopping around. Interest rates vary, and sometimes there are annual fees. Some credit cards offer rewards, like points toward air travel or major purchases.

The good thing about credit cards is that they can let you take advantage of a great sale when you don't have enough in the bank right then. Credit card spending can even be cheaper than using a debit card, as long as bills are paid off every month. Also, monthly credit card statements are a useful record of purchases.

The word "pay" comes from *pacare,* the Latin word meaning "to pacify."

Mail order

Shopping by mail order catalogue can be convenient: instead of slogging around the mall all afternoon, you just turn to the right page and pick out what you want. A quick phone call or trip to the mailbox seals the deal.

But there can be problems. Catalogue pictures don't always show you exactly what you're getting, so you need to read written descriptions very carefully. Check the measurements to make sure the size is right. What's the product made of? How does it compare in quality to other similar items? Read the small print.

Money-saving tip: If your aunt in Nebraska is sending you a gift, make sure she sends it from her home rather than direct from the distributor. Otherwise, you'll have to pay duty on it.

Pay attention to shipping charges and taxes — as well as customs duties and the exchange rate, if you're ordering from outside Canada. You could be in for a shock when you see the bill.

When you place a catalogue order, be careful to provide all the needed information, for the best chance of getting what you want. Measure for size instead of guessing. Make a photocopy of any order you send and keep it on file. Be familiar with the company's return policy, since you're buying sight unseen. And know who to get in touch with in case your order never arrives.

On-line shopping

This is as convenient as catalogue shopping, but a little trickier when it comes to paying. Most on-line stores take credit card numbers directly over the Internet. Security can be an issue, although stores have made great efforts to make sure their customers feel safe keying in their credit card numbers. (A site with "https" or "shttp" in its Web address is a secure site. But this isn't the only way to spot a secure page. You should also check at the bottom of your browser for the "secure" symbol — usually a closed padlock or an unbroken key.)

But credit card shopping isn't an option for most kids. So clever marketing types have come up with a way for kids to safely shop on-line.

On-line shopping portals let parents set up an electronic "wallet" for kids to use. There are several of these sites on the Web, catering to the needs and wants of kids (but for now they're not available to Canadians). Kids can shop at a variety of on-line stores until they've used up the amount in the account, and parents can refresh the account whenever they choose to. Relatives and friends can add money, too, or they can check out a kid's wish list. Parents can sometimes set restrictions on the kind of stuff kids can buy. Sites like RocketCash.com, iCanBuy.com, and DoughNET.com are truly cyber shopping centres for kids.

Be smart: if you ever open an on-line account, be sure to carefully read the privacy policy, and to find out if there are any fees. Also, since most e-stores are from the U.S., the same warnings that apply to catalogue shopping apply here. Keep an eye on the exchange rate, shipping charges, and duties — they can make your shopping experience a bust.

Afterword

We all know what a powerful force money can be. Over the last few thousand years, it's changed the face of the world — and it's changed along with the world.

Understanding money, and knowing how to handle it, puts the power in your hands. And while it's true that having money won't guarantee happiness, using it wisely can help you achieve your goals.

So what are you waiting for? Get out there and prosper!

Web Site Hot List

The Canadian Currency Museum
http://collections.ic.gc.ca/bank/english/index.htm

The Canadian Bankers Association
http://www.cba.ca

The Toronto Stock Exchange
http://tse.com

The Bank of Canada
http://www.bankofcanada.ca/en/index.htm

Bank Notes (Bank of Canada banknote info)
http://www.bankofcanada.ca/en/banknotes/index.html

The Royal Canadian Mint
http://www.rcmint.ca

Numismatic Network Canada
http://www.nunetcan.net

Just for kids:

Youth Resource Network of Canada
http://www.youth.gc.ca

Kidstock
http://www3.kidstock.com

Kids Can Save
http://www.kidscansave.gc.ca

There's Something About Money
http://www.yourmoney.cba.ca

CBC Street Cents Online
http://www.halifax.cbc.ca/streetcents

Zillions Online
http://www.zillions.org

Index